COOKIES

Will and Wisdom

what about
HONESTY?

Art Direction and Design: David Riley Associates, Newport Beach, California Rileydra.com

Published in 2016 by Will and Wisdom Books, Newport Beach, California
and BluSky Publishers, Franklin, Tennessee

ISBN 978-0-9970531-1-1

this book belongs to:

One day, *Will* came home

with *Wisdom* in his backpack.

They had been playing soccer.

Dinner was in the oven but *Will*

was really hungry.

He yelled to his mom who

as upstairs, "Mom, what time

is dinner!?" *Will's* mom yelled

back, "We'll eat at six when

daddy gets home!"

Will looked at the clock. It wasn't even five yet. "I'm not going to be able to make it until six. I think I better eat a cookie." "*Will,* you know you aren't supposed to eat a snack before dinner,"

Wisdom reminded *Will.*

"It's just one cookie," explained *Will*.

"It's no big deal if I eat just one little

cookie. Besides, no one will ever know if

I eat it. The only people here are you and

me and I'm not going to say anything,

are you?" *Will* asked.

"No," admitted *Wisdom.* "I won't tell anyone either." *Will* then grabbed a cookie from the cookie jar and ate it. "Mmm, that was quite tasty. But not very filling. I think I'll need a few more."

༄༄༄

Will reached back into the cookie

jar and pulled out some more cookies.

Wisdom rolled his eyes. "That should

do it," *Will* announced. "That should

do it alright," agreed *Wisdom*.

Finally, it was six o'clock and time for dinner.

Will's mom had made one of Will's favorite

meals, meatloaf. But Will wasn't very hungry.

His father asked, "What's wrong, Will? You love

Mom's meatloaf. Why aren't you eating?" "I guess

I am not very hungry tonight," answered Will.

"Why not?" asked Will's dad.

Suddenly, *Will* realized that if

he told the truth he'd be in big

trouble. "Can I please be excused for

one minute?" *Will* asked. "I will be

right back." *Will* ran upstairs to his

room and asked *Wisdom*

what he should do.

Wisdom rubbed his chin and thought for a moment. Then he said, "You need to be honest and tell the truth." "But if I'm honest I will be in big trouble," explained *Will.*

"Probably," agreed *Wisdom.*

"But one of God's Ten Commandments in

the Bible tells us that we are not supposed

to lie. So, if we are not honest we are

not obeying God."

Will knew that *Wisdom* was right.

He went back downstairs and told his parents

the truth. *Will's* dad punished him for eating

the cookies but he also gave him a big hug for

being honest and telling the truth.

THE END

Do not lie.

Leviticus 19:11

℮℮℮

A truthful witness gives

honest testimony.

Proverbs 12:17

A Prayer To Follow God
and Become a Christian

Dear God,

Help me to be honest and do the right things.
I believe you love me so much that you gave your
only Son, Jesus, to die on the cross for the things
that I have done wrong. Please forgive me and
come into my life and change me. I believe that
Jesus rose from the dead and is coming back some
day. Until then, I will follow you for the rest of my
life. Jesus is my God, my Savior and my forever
Friend. In Jesus' Name, Amen.

_____   _____
your name   date

If you have just prayed that prayer and meant it with all your heart, you are a child of God and will live with Him forever in heaven.

Here's what you can do now:

1. Read the Bible to learn more about God.

2. Go to church and worship with other believers.

3. Be baptized so that others know of your commitment to follow God.

4. Pray everyday and thank the Lord for all that you have.

5. Know that you can do and accomplish anything with God in your life.